FOR
LITTLE PETER
IN
NEW ZEALAND

FREDERICK WARNE

Published by the Penguin Group
Registered office: 80 Strand, London, WC2R ORL
Penguin Young Readers Group, 345 Hudson Street, New York, N.Y. 10014, USA

First published 1922 by Frederick Warne
This edition with new reproductions of Beatrix Potter's book illustrations first published 2007
This edition copyright © Frederick Warne & Co. 2007
New reproductions of Beatrix Potter's book illustrations copyright © Frederick Warne & Co. 2002
Original copyright in text and illustrations © Frederick Warne & Co., 1922

Manufactured in China

Cecily Parsley's Nursery Rhymes

by Beatrix Potter

FREDERICK WARNE

CECILY PARSLEY
lived in a pen,
And brewed good ale
for gentlemen;

GENTLEMEN
came every day,
Till Cecily Parsley
ran away.

8

Goosey, goosey, gander,
Whither will you wander?
Upstairs and downstairs,
And in my lady's chamber!

THIS pig went to market;
This pig stayed at home;

THIS pig had a bit of meat;

AND this pig had none;

THIS little pig cried
    Wee! wee! wee!
I can't find my way home.

17

18

PUSSY-CAT sits by the fire;
    How should she be fair?
In walks the little dog,
    Says "Pussy! are you there?"

"HOW do you do, Mistress Pussy?
Mistress Pussy, how do you do?"
"I thank you kindly, little dog,
I fare as well as you!"

THREE blind mice, three blind mice,
See how they run!
They all run after the farmer's wife,
And she cut off their tails
with a carving knife,
Did ever you see such a thing
in your life
As three blind mice!

B OW, WOW, WOW!
Whose dog art thou?
"I'm little Tom Tinker's dog,
Bow, wow, wow!"

WE have a little garden,
  A garden of our own,
And every day we water there
  The seeds that we have sown.

WE love our little garden,
     And tend it with such care,
You will not find a faded leaf
     Or blighted blossom there.

NINNY NANNY NETTICOAT,
In a white petticoat,
With a red nose —
The longer she stands,
The shorter she grows.